The Adventure Begins . . .

Hi! I'm Jackie. I love adventure. That's why I'm an archaeologist. My job is to search the world for ancient treasure. I study it to learn how people lived in the past.

Last month I read about a crazy king named Mad King Ludwig. He lived in a castle in Bavaria, Germany, a long time ago.

People said that he had a huge roomful of treasure hidden somewhere in his crumbling castle.

Not everybody believed the story. But I did.

I traveled all the way from my home in San Francisco, California, to King Ludwig's castle in Bavaria. I wanted to find out the truth.

I thought it would be a simple treasure hunt.

But I was wrong.

It was the beginning of the most amazing adventure ever—and it all started with a golden shield . . .

A PARACHUTE PRESS BOOK

Published by Grosset & Dunlap, a division of Penguin Putnam Books for Young Readers, New York. GROSSET & DUNLAP is a trademark of Penguin Putnam, Inc. Published simultaneously in Canada. Printed in U.S.A.

Library of Congress Cataloging-in-Publication Data is available.

ISBN 0-448-42649-8
A B C D E F G H I J

JACKIE CHAN ADVENTURES™ #1

The Dark Hand

A novelization by Eliza Willard
based on the teleplay "The Dark Hand"
written by John Rodgers

Grosset & Dunlap

Chapter 1

"It's not a very cozy home, is it?" Jackie Chan said to his two assistants, Skip and Maryann.

He stared up at the old, crumbling castle in front of him. It sat on top of a steep, rocky mountain. Its pointed towers rose high into the air.

Jackie was an archaeologist—a scientist who searched the world for ancient treasures. He and his team were in Bavaria. They hoped to find the lost fortune of Mad King Ludwig.

Jackie, Skip, and Maryann entered the castle. It was dark and cold inside. Jackie beamed his flashlight over the stone walls. He had a hunch that the famous treasure was right under his nose. But he knew there was danger nearby, too.

"Mad King Ludwig lived in this castle hundreds of years ago," Jackie explained. "The king often set deadly traps for his visitors."

"That's no way to treat a guest," Skip said. He tugged on his red cap.

"That's why he was called '*Mad* King Ludwig' and not 'Kind and Friendly' King of Bavaria,'" Jackie joked.

Jackie stopped suddenly. He gave

a signal for the others to a halt.

He pulled a can of spray paint from his backpack. He sprayed a white mist into the air.

When the mist settled, Jackie pointed to a very thin wire. It hung between two stone walls. It had been invisible in the dark, but the white paint made it show up.

"Wow!" Maryann gasped. "How did you spot that?"

"Stand back," Jackie warned her. He snatched the red cap from Skip's head. Then he carefully dropped the hat onto the wire.

Two huge blocks of stone jolted out of the walls. They slammed together with a bang! Then they quickly pulled apart again.

Skip gulped. “That could have crushed us!”

“It’s safe now,” Jackie said.

As they crept forward, Jackie searched for more traps and for clues to the treasure. Soon he found a heavy stone door.

Jackie studied the door carefully. A skull sat on the floor beside it. Jackie stuck his fingers into the skull’s empty eye sockets and pulled.

The door slid up into the ceiling.

Jackie and his team stepped through the entrance. They found themselves in a large, dark room.

Jackie lit a torch that hung on a wall. The room flooded with light. Skip and Maryann gasped.

The light gleamed off stacks of

coins, jewels, suits of armor, and antique weapons.

"Ludwig's lost treasure!" Maryann cried. "We found it!"

"Wow!" Skip shouted. He began to move toward the riches.

Jackie glanced around the room. "I'm sure the treasure is booby-trapped," he warned. "So don't—"

Before Jackie could finish, Skip picked up a small jeweled statue.

"—touch anything," Jackie said with a sigh.

Suddenly, the room began to shake.

Jackie spun around to see the stone door sliding shut.

I can't let that door close, he thought. *Or we'll be trapped here forever!*

Chapter 2

Jackie grabbed a silver spear and threw it up into the air. Whirling around, he kicked the spear across the room. It landed in the doorway, its pointed end stuck in the ground.

The stone door hit the top of the spear and stopped. But Jackie knew the spear wouldn't hold the heavy door open for long.

Skip and Maryann stood frozen in place. They stared at the door as the room shook around them.

"Run!" Jackie shouted.

The pair scurried out of the room to safety. But when Jackie reached the door—

Crack! The spear snapped in half.

The stone door slammed shut with a crash. Jackie was trapped inside the treasure room!

"Bad day," he muttered.

Then dozens of arrows shot toward him out of the walls!

Jackie ducked and rolled. The arrows whizzed past him. He dove toward a pile of treasure and grabbed a golden shield. Arrows clanked off the shield as he ran through the room. "Bad-day-bad-day-bad-day!" he cried.

High overhead Jackie spotted a narrow hole in one wall.

A way out!

Still clutching the shield, he leaped up the wall to the opening. He slipped through the gap—

And tumbled down a steep ramp!

Then he flew out the side of the castle! "Ahhhhhhhh!" Jackie sailed though the air on the shield.

The shield landed with a thud on the side of the mountain. Jackie slid down the rocky mountainside, grunting with every bump.

At last he came to a stop at the entrance to the castle.

Maryann and Skip were waiting for him there. They stared at him with their mouths open.

Jackie stood up and tucked the shield under his arm. "Sledding works much better on snow," he said with a grin.

High up on the mountain, someone was watching Jackie and his team. He was a thin man with ice-blue eyes and a long blond ponytail.

He looked at Jackie through a pair of binoculars.

Three tough guys stood nearby. They were ready to carry out the blond man's orders.

The man stared at the shield as Jackie carried it down the mountain. He turned to his three enforcers.

"Follow him," the man ordered.

Chapter 3

Two days later, Jackie was back home in San Francisco. Jackie lived in an apartment above his uncle's antique shop.

"Hah! Hah! Hah! Hah!" Jackie shouted. He was practicing kicks on a punching bag in his training room.

The room was filled with martial arts equipment and photos from Jackie's adventures around the world.

A bell near the ceiling jangled.

Uncle needs me, Jackie thought. Uncle always rang the bell when he needed Jackie.

Jackie stopped practicing and hurried downstairs to the antique shop.

The store was called Uncle's Rare Finds. It was packed with old statues, vases, swords, and furniture.

Jackie's uncle stood behind a desk. He was a short man with gray hair and glasses. He studied the shield Jackie had brought back from Bavaria.

Uncle smiled when he saw Jackie. "Come give Uncle a hug."

Jackie moved toward his uncle with open arms. But just as Jackie was about to give him a hug, Uncle whacked him on the forehead.

“Ow!” Jackie cried, rubbing his head. “What was that for?”

“You did not make coffee this morning!” Uncle scolded him. “Coffee is the only thing keeping Uncle’s ancient heart beating! You want dead Uncle?”

Jackie shook his head no.

“Then you make coffee!” Uncle added.

“Okay.” Jackie turned toward the kitchen.

“One more thing.” Uncle said, stopping Jackie.

He pointed to the shield on his desk. An eight-sided gray stone with a picture of a red rooster on it was set in the shield’s center. The stone looked like a talisman—a magical charm. Ancient Chinese words were scratched onto the shield.

"I cannot read these writings," Uncle complained. "They're very old. I must go in the back and look at my journals."

"Okay," Jackie repeated. He took another step toward the kitchen.

"One *more* thing," Uncle added.

Jackie sighed. "What is it?"

"This is Jade, your niece. She will live with you for one year, okay?" Uncle asked.

"Okay," Jackie said without thinking. One more time he turned to leave—then stopped. *"What?"*

He whirled around to face Uncle. For the first time Jackie noticed a small girl standing in a corner of the room. She was surrounded by suitcases. She wore a red sweatshirt, baggy jeans, and a frown on her face.

"I have a *niece?*" Jackie asked. He'd never heard about her before.

Uncle rested a hand on Jackie's shoulder. "Jade is your cousin Shin's girl from Hong Kong. She was not behaving well there. Doing poorly in school. Your cousin thinks she will do better in America, with you."

"But nobody asked *me!*" Jackie said.

"We did not want to bother you," Uncle explained. He picked up the shield. "Now you both get to know each other while I go and work." He pulled aside the curtain that led to the back room of the store.

"But I don't know anything about children!" Jackie cried. How could he take care of a little girl?

Uncle disappeared behind the curtain without another word.

Jackie stared at Jade. Does she speak English? he wondered. Better talk slowly, just in case.

"Hello," he said. "I . . . am . . . Jackie."

Jade stared back at him. She did not say a word.

Guess she doesn't speak English after all, Jackie thought.

He was glad when the shop door opened.

Three men walked in. The first man had red hair and wore a white suit. The second had black hair and wore orange sunglasses. The third was a beefy man with a greenish face like Frankenstein's.

"Welcome to Uncle's Rare Finds," Jackie said. "How can I help you?"

"Are you Jackie Chan?" the first guy asked.

Jackie nodded. He gave the man a friendly smile.

The man did not smile back. "We are aware that you recently found a shield in a Bavarian castle. Our very rich boss wants to buy that shield."

Jackie glanced from one man to the next. He noticed their big fists and flashy clothes. Clearly they were thugs—tough guys who were *not* friendly.

Jackie did not trust them. "I'm

sorry," he said. "I already gave that piece to a museum."

"I suggest you get it back," the first man said.

The greenish man flicked a huge hand at a priceless vase on a table. It wobbled and fell toward the floor.

In a flash, Jackie moved to catch the falling vase. He saved it just in time.

The first man frowned. Then he turned and patted Jade on the head.

"Get the shield back, Mr. Chan," he said, "by this time tomorrow. Or you and your family . . . will pay."

Chapter 4

The three men left the store.

Uncle came out from the back room. “Did they buy anything?”

“No,” Jackie said. He pulled on a jacket. “Watch the girl, and hide the shield,” he told Uncle.

He did not know who those thugs were, but he was going to find out. Why did they threaten his family? Why was the shield so important?

Jackie hurried out into the street.

He saw the men climb into a long white car and pull away.

Jackie scurried up a fire escape to the roof of a nearby building. He leaped from roof to roof, following the car as it moved through the streets. The car stopped at a red light.

I need a much closer look, Jackie thought. He spotted a narrow drain-pipe attached to the building. He started to slide down it.

But Jackie was too heavy. The top end of the pipe broke loose from the building.

"Whoa!" Jackie cried. The pipe swerved out over the cars on the street. Then it snapped off the wall!

"Aaaahh!" Jackie crashed onto the hood of the white car.

The thugs inside the car jumped when they saw Jackie.

"Oops." Jackie smiled. Then he rolled off the car and ran.

The thugs chased Jackie into a playground. A group of children were on the swings.

"No more playtime!" he called to the kids. "Go, go, go!"

The children ran out of the park to safety. The three thugs rushed to fight Jackie.

Jackie twirled and kicked and blocked their punches. He yanked a tetherball with all his might, then let it fly. It swung around its pole and knocked the biggest guy in the head.

The other two thugs charged him.

But Jackie tangled them up in the swings.

The three thugs dragged themselves to their feet, moaning in pain. "Let's get out of here," one said. They turned and ran back to their car.

Jackie watched the car peel away. He brushed the dirt from his hands. Then he noticed a girl who was standing nearby. It's Jade, he realized. She followed me!

Jade opened her mouth to say something.

Suddenly, a tall, bald man in a black coat stepped out from behind a tree. He held up a can, and sprayed a green mist into Jackie's face.

Jackie moaned and fell to the ground. Everything went black.

Chapter 5

"He's waking up."

Jackie heard a man's voice. He opened his eyes and blinked. He found himself in the back of a van.

The van was moving. The tall, bald man leaned over Jackie. Two other men waited behind him.

Jackie let out a cry of surprise. "Augustus Black!" he shouted. "What are you doing here?" He sat up and threw his arms around the bald man.

Captain Augustus Black was an old friend of Jackie's. He was the head of a top secret law enforcement agency.

Jackie suddenly felt dizzy. He leaned back on the floor. "What am *I* doing here?" he asked.

"I'm afraid it's official business," Captain Black said.

Jackie glanced at the two agents with Black. "I didn't think these were your backup singers," he joked. "Where have you been? I haven't heard from you in six years. Now all of a sudden you show up and save my life?"

He rubbed the sore spot on his head. "Those thugs must have knocked me out," he added.

"Actually, *I* knocked you out," Black admitted.

"You?" Jackie asked. He was shocked.

The van slowed to a stop. Jackie leaped to his feet and jumped out. Captain Black followed.

"Why did you do that?" Jackie demanded. "I thought we were friends!"

"We are, Jackie," Black said. "I'm sorry, but this place must remain secret. I *had* to do it."

Jackie looked around. They were in a narrow alley. A phone booth stood against one wall. Garbage cans were lined up nearby.

"Yes, I can see that this is some very special garbage," he snapped.

"Excuse me while I call a cab."

Jackie stepped into the phone booth and slammed the door shut.

"Uh, Jackie . . ." Black started to say.

Jackie didn't hear anything else. The phone booth was sucked through a hole in the wall!

As fast as a speeding car, it zipped down a long hallway.

"Whoa!" Jackie cried. He clung to the glass sides as the booth headed straight for a concrete wall!

Clunk! The phone booth stopped inches from the wall. Jackie let out a shaky breath.

But then the booth dropped through a hole in the floor. Jackie screamed as it fell down.

Finally it stopped falling. The door slid open, and Jackie tumbled out.

He found Captain Black waiting for him.

"I tried to warn you," Black said.

"How did you get down here?" Jackie asked.

"The stairs," Captain Black replied. "Follow me."

He led Jackie through a door marked with the number thirteen. They stood on a metal catwalk overlooking a huge room.

There were hundreds of people below them. They were working in front of video screens. Jackie was amazed. All of this was hidden behind an alley!

"Jackie, welcome to Section Thirteen," Black announced.

"You're a *spy?*" Jackie asked. He stared at the people milling about below him. "*They're* spies?"

Black shook his head no. "Law enforcement, Jackie. Elite special forces."

"Elite special forces?" Jackie repeated. He thought it over. "So why give *me* the big tour?"

"We are aware that you found a shield in Bavaria," Black told him.

Jackie couldn't believe his ears. "You're the second one to ask me about that shield today," he told his friend. "Tell me what's going on."

Black led Jackie to a big TV screen, hanging on a wall. "Section

Thirteen has stopped some very serious crimes," he explained. "Most of these crimes were done by a group called The Dark Hand."

The words *Dark Hand* appeared on the TV screen.

"These are extremely dangerous people," Black continued. "Their leader is this man—Valmont."

Valmont's face came on the screen. He had ice-blue eyes, a sharp chin, and a long blond ponytail.

Jackie looked at him carefully. He knew that one day he would come face to face with this man.

At that very moment, Valmont stood in his fancy office. He listened to a report from his three enforcers.

"Are you telling me that *one man* stopped you?" Valmont demanded.

"Uh . . . yes?" the red-haired thug said.

Valmont glared at them. He knew someone who could teach these idiots a lesson. "Tohru!" he called.

A giant man stepped out of the shadows. He was bigger than all three enforcers put together.

The enforcers turned and saw Tohru. Their faces fell. They began to shake with terror.

Tohru reached down and picked them up. His arms tightened around them . . . and squeezed.

The three enforcers kicked and squirmed. "Help!" they groaned. "Can't . . . breathe . . ."

Valmont smirked. He liked to see people get punished. Finally, he signaled for Tohru to stop. "Enough," he said.

Tohru dropped the enforcers. They collapsed to the ground, and gasped for air.

"Tohru, bring me the shield," Valmont ordered.

Behind Valmont, a stone sculpture hung on the wall. It had the face of a dragon, with red jewels for eyes.

The spirit of Shendu lived inside the statue. Shendu was the real leader of The Dark Hand.

The red eyes on the sculpture glowed. Then a creepy voice came from the statue.

"While your Tohru is very good at

his job, Valmont," the dragon hissed, "perhaps he should be helped by . . . the Shadowkhan."

As Shendu spoke, dozens of ninjas flitted like bats out of the shadows. The warriors were dressed in black from head to toe. Their eyes glowed red—just like those of the dragon.

"As you wish, Shendu," Valmont said. "I will do whatever it takes to get that shield—and to get rid of Jackie Chan."

Chapter 6

"We just found out that The Dark Hand has a new interest," Captain Black told Jackie at Section Thirteen. "They are collecting many historical artifacts."

"Why?" Jackie asked.

"We don't know. But you may be able to help us find out. We could use an archaeology expert like you."

Jackie wasn't certain. Getting involved with The Dark Hand could be dangerous. And now he had a little girl to take care of.

"It wouldn't be full-time, Jackie," Black said. "You just have to do research. To help us stay one step ahead of Valmont."

"I'll think about it," Jackie agreed.

The roar of an engine interrupted them. A motor scooter zoomed down the hallway. It was out of control. Agents were running after it.

The scooter zipped past Jackie and Captain Black. Jackie couldn't believe who was riding it—Jade!

"Jaaackiiieeee!" Jade screamed as she flashed past them.

The scooter spun around and headed back toward Jackie.

Thinking quickly, Jackie grabbed

a rolling office chair. He set one knee on it. Then he grabbed Jade's sleeve as she roared past him.

Jackie rolled on the chair beside Jade as the scooter pulled him along. He reached for the ignition switch and turned the power off.

The scooter skidded to a stop. But Jackie and the chair rolled past it—and crashed into a pile of boxes!

"Oomph!" Jackie sat up on the floor, dazed from the crash.

"Let go of me!" he heard Jade cry.

Jackie shook off his daze. She *does* speak English, he realized. He saw Jade struggling with two agents.

"Young lady, how did you get in here?" Captain Black demanded.

"The stairs," Jade said.

Jackie marched over to her. "Where did you get the motorbike?" he asked. "You could have been hurt!"

Jade leaned close to Jackie. "I sneaked it out of their garage," she whispered. "I knew we'd need it to get out of here."

"Jade, these people are my friends," Jackie explained.

Jade stared at Jackie. "Your *friends* knocked you out and took you to a secret underground base?"

"Uh . . . yes," Jackie answered.

Jade grinned. "America is *so* cool!"

Black turned to one of the agents. "How did a *child* break through our security?" he asked in an angry voice.

"I'm not a child!" Jade insisted.

Jackie pulled Jade aside to scold

her. But before he could speak, she said, "Come on, admit it. Wasn't I brave?"

"Yes," Jackie admitted. "But you also need wisdom. You need to know when challenges are too big. Courage without wisdom is foolishness. Do you understand?"

Just then, Jackie's cell phone rang. He pulled it out of his pocket and said, "Hello?"

"Jackie!" He heard Uncle's voice. "Where are you?"

Jackie's eyes darted to Black. "Uh, can't say," Jackie told Uncle. Jackie knew he couldn't tell anyone about Section Thirteen.

"Oh," Uncle said. "One more thing. Have you seen Jade?"

"Yes, she's with me," Jackie said.

"See? I knew you two would get along," Uncle said. "One *more* thing. I have been doing research on the shield from Bavaria. I have found what the writings on it mean. They tell of magic. Very powerful. But shield not important."

"Of *course* the shield is important!" Jackie cried. "Everybody I meet today wants the shield!"

"Nah," Uncle said. "Shield not important."

Then Jackie heard a deep, scary voice talking to Uncle. "Give me the shield," the voice said.

"Uncle?" Jackie called into the phone. "Uncle? Uncle!"

Uncle didn't answer.

Chapter 7

"Uncle! Uncle! Answer me!" Jackie shouted into the phone. He was really worried.

Then he heard the deep voice say, "This is Tohru. Your uncle is fine for now, Mr. Chan. But he won't be if I don't get the shield."

"I understand," Jackie said.

Tohru told Jackie to bring the shield to the Nokashiro Building. It was a huge skyscraper in downtown

San Francisco. "And tell no one—or your uncle is doomed."

Jackie clicked off his cell phone. He turned to Black. "I must ask you a favor. Please watch my niece for a while."

"Jackie," Black said. "Where are you going?"

"Please, don't ask questions," Jackie said. He hurried to the exit. The door slid open. Jackie stepped back into the phone booth and was whooshed up to the street.

Jackie rushed back to his uncle's shop. He glanced around the cluttered store. "Where would Uncle hide the shield?"

He picked up an old screen to move it aside.

"Hi!" Jade smiled up at him from behind the screen.

Startled, Jackie jumped and grabbed his chest. "Aaahhh!"

"How did you . . . ?" he began to ask Jade.

"The stairs," she answered with a shrug.

Jackie pointed at the steps leading up to his apartment. "Well, take *those* stairs up to your room."

"Aw, let me help," Jade whined. "Uncle is my uncle, too."

Jackie watched her face closely. He had a feeling she wouldn't go to her room, no matter what he said.

"Fine," he agreed. "Help me find the shield."

He turned away from her to start

searching. He piled up items on a small table. Jade pulled the top of the table out from under the pile.

"Yahh-hah!" she shouted.

All the items flew into the air—and landed in a heap on top of Jackie. He poked his head out of the pile, ready to scold her.

But she held up the tabletop for him to see. "Is this it?" she asked.

Jackie recognized the shield. "Yes!" he cried.

Jade smiled. "I must be getting some of that wisdom stuff you were talking about."

Jackie took the shield away from her. He headed for the door. "Thank you. Now go to your room."

He didn't have time to make sure

she obeyed. He had to get to the Nokashiro Building before Uncle got hurt.

Jackie hurried downtown. Soon he found himself at the foot of the big skyscraper. He glanced around, searching for the entrance.

A girl's voice sounded behind him. "Uncle's up there, huh?" Jade said.

Jackie whirled around, stunned. How could such a little girl be so bad?

"Do you speak English?" he demanded.

"You know I do," she answered.

"So what part of 'Go to your room' do you not understand?"

"Aw . . . ," Jade pouted.

"Stay here," Jackie ordered. "Or I'll put you on the first plane back to Hong Kong!"

Jackie turned and ran into the building. He rode the elevator to the very top of the building. He stepped out onto the roof.

Jackie saw a giant man in the moonlight. Tohru.

Tohru stood near another door leading to a second flight of stairs. Uncle was huddled beside him. A scarf was tied around Uncle's mouth. His hands were tied, too.

"The shield," Tohru commanded. "Give it to me."

Jackie wasn't sure. He would do anything to save Uncle. But even if he gave Tohru the golden shield, would Uncle really be safe?

"Why does your boss want it?" Jackie asked.

"That is not your concern," Tohru replied.

Out of the corner of his eye, Jackie saw something move. The door to the stairs cracked open. Jade's head peeked out.

What is she doing here? Jackie thought angrily. Then he realized she might be able to help.

Jackie stared at Jade. Then he darted his eyes toward Uncle. He hoped that Jade would understand his signal.

Jade nodded. Now Jackie had to set up a distraction.

He shouted to Tohru, "You want

the shield? Catch!" He tossed the shield toward Tohru. It floated high over the giant man's head.

Tohru reached for it and missed. The shield sailed off the edge of the skyscraper.

But then, like a boomerang, it spun around and reversed its course. It zoomed over Tohru's head again and landed neatly in Jackie's arms.

"Fool!" Tohru shouted. "Say good-bye to Uncle!" He turned to strike Uncle with a massive fist.

But Uncle was not there. Jackie watched as Jade and Uncle slipped through the door to the stairs.

Tohru growled with rage.

Jackie raced toward the elevator with the shield.

Then he heard something flutter through the air behind him. He turned to see what it was. But there was nothing was behind him.

Then he heard the noise again. It sounded like bats diving through the air. Jackie spun around.

Suddenly, he was surrounded by a dozen ninjas—the Shadowkhan. They were dressed all in black. Their red eyes glowed as they stared at the shield.

Jackie glanced at the shield. "You want this?" he asked. Again he tossed the shield—just like a boomerang. It floated toward the edge of the roof.

The Shadowkhan chased after it. One leaped up to catch the shield as it returned.

Jackie tripped him, and the ninja missed. Jackie reached out and caught the shield.

He quickly ran across the roof. The Shadowkhan followed, throwing sharp ninja stars at him.

Jackie held up the shield. The ninja stars bounced off it.

"Whoa!" Jackie skidded to a stop. He had reached the edge of the roof. He turned to face the scary ninjas. Now what was he going to do?

Behind him was a ninety-floor drop. In front of him loomed the Shadowkhan. They moved toward him, closer and closer. . . .

Jackie had no choice. He turned around and leaped off the roof!

Chapter 8

Jackie landed lightly on a ledge ten floors below.

The Shadowkhan followed. They swung along the skyscraper wall as easily as spiders. Two jumped ahead of him. Two landed behind him.

Jackie looked around. He was trapped. He spotted Jade and Uncle far, far below him. They stood outside the building, gazing up at Jackie.

"Jackie!" Jade called.

The Shadowkhan inched toward Jackie from every direction. There's no way out, Jackie realized. He knew what he had to do.

Jackie tossed the shield over the edge of the building. It whooshed gently down to the ground—straight toward Jade and Uncle.

The shield landed safely in Jade's arms.

Then Jackie saw Tohru come out of the building. Jackie's heart sank.

Tohru walked slowly toward Jade and Uncle. Uncle shouted and gave Tohru a fierce karate kick.

Tohru didn't blink. The kick didn't hurt him at all! He held out his hands for the shield.

Jade handed it over to him.

Jackie sighed. He knew she had no choice.

The Shadowkhan fluttered around him. Then they disappeared into the shadows. Tohru had the shield. Their mission was over.

Suddenly, spotlights flooded the ledge. A helicopter approached the side of the building. The wind from its blades blew Jackie's hair and clothes.

Captain Black waved from the helicopter. He threw Jackie a rope ladder. Jackie climbed aboard.

A few minutes later they landed in front of the building.

Jackie and Captain Black got out of the helicopter.

"Jackie, I never meant for your

family to get involved in this," Black apologized.

"It's not your fault," Jackie said. "The Dark Hand was after the golden shield."

Uncle rapped Jackie across the forehead with his fingers.

"Ow!" Jackie cried.

"I told you, shield not important!" Uncle insisted. "Talisman in the center of shield *is*. It is a magical charm. It is very powerful."

"Don't worry," Black said to Uncle. "We'll get the talisman back from The Dark Hand."

"Don't need to," Jade said. She pulled something out of her pocket.

Inside her hand was the rooster talisman!

Jade winked at Jackie. "Admit it," she said. "I'm getting wise."

Meanwhile, back at The Dark Hand headquarters, Tohru bowed to Valmont. Valmont was standing beside Shendu.

"For you, master," Tohru said. He gave Valmont the shield.

Valmont stared at the hole in its center—the hole where the talisman should have been.

Shendu's red eyes flashed angrily.

"You fool!" Valmont cried. "Where is the talisman?"

Uncle took the talisman from Jade's hand. "One more thing," he said. "See the markings?" He pointed to the red rooster. "Sign of the Rooster, from the Chinese zodiac."

Jackie stared at the talisman.

"There are twelve signs in the Chinese zodiac," Uncle went on. "So somewhere there are eleven more talismans."

"And something tells me The Dark Hand is after all of them," Black said. "Will you help us, Jackie?"

Before he could answer, Jade cried out, "Absolutely!"

What could Jackie say? His niece was right. He couldn't turn down Captain Black. Not with The Dark Hand after the other talismans. He had to help—no matter what the danger!

A letter to you from Jackie

Dear Friends,

In *The Dark Hand*, Jade wants to show me she's tough and brave, but I tell her a secret about life. Courage without wisdom is foolishness.

Kids always ask me, "Jackie, how can you be so brave?" They see me fight off the tough guys from The Dark Hand in JACKIE CHAN ADVENTURES. They see me jump off buildings and onto cars in my movies. They think I'm not afraid of danger. They couldn't be more wrong.

Naturally, I am scared when I do dangerous things. But I never do them foolishly. I learn about the risks, I practice, and I am very prepared. Real courage comes from wisdom, not from outrageous actions.

In one of my movies I did a big scene in a shark tank—with a man-eating shark! It was very scary when the shark swam close to me. But I wasn't really afraid. Why not? Because I took the time to learn everything I needed to know about sharks. I listened to a shark expert before I entered the tank. He showed me a special light I could use to keep the shark away if I needed to. And he showed me just what to do if the shark came close.

I remember another time when I needed courage. I was facing a dangerous situation. Everyone was waiting for me to jump in and save the day. But I wasn't sure I had figured out what to do. So do you know what I did?

Nothing.

That's right, I sat down and thought about it. I thought for two whole days until I felt sure I had the right plan. I waited until I knew what I was doing before I took such a big risk.

It was very hard to sit there and know that everyone was thinking I was crazy or scared. But I knew it would be foolish to do something dangerous just because I was afraid of what people might say about me.

Have you ever been in that situation? Maybe someone dared you to do something that you weren't sure you could do. Did you have the wisdom to say no to the dare? If that happens again—remember this. Sometimes it takes more courage to do nothing than to do the most dangerous act. And that's another one of life's little secrets!

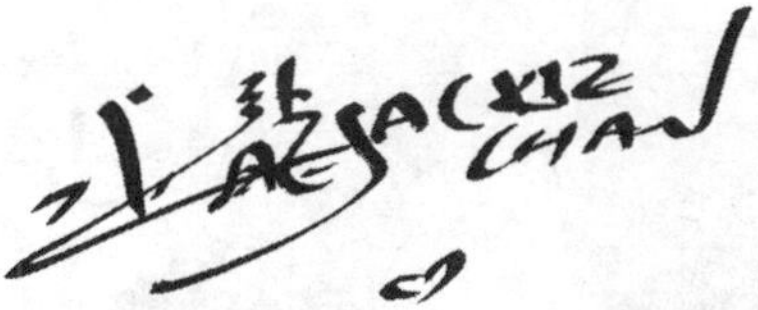

Find out what happens in the next book

#2 Jade's Secret Power

Jackie finds the rooster talisman—and then loses it! What will it take to get it back?

JACKIE CHAN ADVENTURES™

Enter the

JACKIE CHAN ADVENTURES™

Ultimate Fan Sweepstakes!

— NO PURCHASE NECESSARY —

Are you the Ultimate Fan?

Enter today and you could be a lucky winner of one of the following great *Jackie Chan Adventures* prizes:

1 Grand Prize

Win a *Jackie Chan Adventures* Ultimate Fan Gift Pack!
Includes the first five Jackie Chan Adventures books autographed by Jackie Chan, T-shirt, video, action figures, sticker activity pack, board game, backpack, video game, and other cool *Jackie Chan Adventures* gifts!

5 First Prizes

Win the first five *Jackie Chan Adventures* books, including an autographed copy of #1 THE DARK HAND!

50 Second Prizes

Win a copy of *Jackie Chan Adventures* #5 SHENDU ESCAPES!

Complete this entry form or hand print all of the information listed below on a 3' x 5' card (see Official Rule #2) and send it to:

Jackie Chan Adventures Ultimate Fan Sweepstakes
Village Station
P. O. Box 1045
New York, NY 10014

Name ______________________________

Address ______________________________

City ______________________________

State ______________ **Zip** ______________

Phone ______________ **Birthdate** ___/___/___

Jackie Chan Adventures™ Ultimate Fan Sweepstakes
Official Rules

1. **NO PURCHASE NECESSARY**. A purchase will not improve your chances of winning.

2. To enter complete the official entry form or hand print your name, address, age, and phone number along with the words "JACKIE CHAN ADVENTURES Ultimate Fan Sweepstakes" on a 3" x 5" card and mail to: JACKIE CHAN ADVENTURES Ultimate Fan Sweepstakes, Village Station, P. O. Box 1045, New York, NY 10014, postmarked **no later than January 31, 2002**. Enter as often as you wish, but each entry must be mailed separately. One entry per envelope. Partially completed, illegible, or mechanically reproduced entries will not be accepted. Sponsor is not responsible for lost, late, mutilated, illegible, stolen, postage due, incomplete, or misdirected entries. All entries become the property of Penguin Putnam Inc., and will not be returned.

3. The sweepstakes is open to legal residents of the United States and Canada (excluding Quebec), between the ages of five and twelve as of January 31, 2002, except as set forth below. Void in Puerto Rico and wherever prohibited or restricted by law. All federal, state, and local laws apply. In the event a winner is a Canadian resident, he or she must answer a time-limited skill question consisting of an arithmetical problem to be determined a winner. Sony Pictures Entertainment Inc., Kids' WB!, Adelaide Productions, Inc., Penguin Putnam Inc., Parachute Properties and Parachute Press, Inc. (individually and collectively "Parachute"), their respective officers, directors, shareholders, employees, suppliers, parents, subsidiaries, affiliates, agencies, sponsors, participating retailers, and persons connected with the use, marketing or conduct of this sweepstakes are not eligible. And family members living in the same household as any of the individuals referred to in the immediately forgoing sentence are not eligible.

4. Odds of winning depend on the total number of entries received. All prizes will be awarded. Winners will be randomly drawn on or about February 15, 2002, by Penguin Putnam Inc., whose decisions are final. Potential winners will be notified by mail and will be required to sign and return an affidavit of eligibility, release of liability, and all other legal documents which the sweepstakes sponsor may require (including a W-9 tax form) within 14 days of notification or an alternate winner will be selected. Prizes won by minors will be awarded to their parent or legal guardian who must sign and return all required legal documents. By acceptance of their prize, winners or winners' parents on winners' behalf consent to the use of their names, photographs, likeness, and personal information by Penguin Putnam, Parachute, Sony Pictures Entertainment, Adelaide, or Kids' WB!, and for any advertising, promotion, or publicity purposes without further compensation except where prohibited.

5. a) One (1) **Grand Prize Winner** wins a JACKIE CHAN ADVENTURES Ultimate Fan Gift Pack which includes the first five JACKIE CHAN ADVENTURES books autographed by Jackie Chan, T-shirt, video, action figures, board game, sticker activity pack, backpack, video game and other Jackie Chan Adventures product. Approximate retail value $100.00.

b) Five (5) **First Prize Winners** win the first five JACKIE CHAN ADVENTURES books, including an autographed copy of Book #1 THE DARK HAND. Approximate retail value $24.95.

c) Fifty (50) **Second Prize Winners** win a copy of JACKIE CHAN ADVENTURES Book #5 SHENDU ESCAPES. Approximate retail value $4.99.

6. Only one prize will be awarded per individual, family, or household. Prizes are non-transferable and cannot be sold or redeemed for cash. No cash substitute is available. Any federal, state, or local taxes are the responsibility of the winner. Sponsor may substitute prize of equal or greater value, if necessary, due to availability.

7. Additional terms: By participating, entrants agree a) to the official rules and decisions of the judges, which will be final in all respects; and to waive any claim to ambiguity of the official rules and b) to release, discharge, and hold harmless Penguin Putnam, Parachute, Sony Pictures Entertainment, Kids' WB!, Adelaide and their respective officers, directors, shareholders, employees, suppliers, parents, subsidiaries, affiliates, agencies, sponsors, participating retailers and persons connected with the use, marketing or conduct of this sweepstakes from and against any and all liability or damages associated with acceptance, use, or misuse of any prize received in this sweepstakes.

8. Any dispute arising from this sweepstakes will be determined according to the laws of the State of New York, without reference to its conflict of law principles, and the entrants consent to the personal jurisdiction of the State and Federal courts located in New York County and agree that such courts have exclusive jurisdiction over all such disputes.

9. To obtain the name of the winners, please send your request and a self-addressed stamped envelope to JACKIE CHAN ADVENTURES Ultimate Fan Sweepstakes, Village Station, P. O. Box 1045, New York, NY 10014 by March 1, 2002. Sweepstakes Sponsor: Penguin Putnam Inc.